C46 0000 0443 321

Don't Look Back!

en Perce, Andy, Eddie and Well'ard go on a school trip London, they don't expect to find the most famous sician in Ancient Greece busking in a tube station. heir plans for the day don't include joining him on a ey down into the darkest reaches of the Underworld to rescue his wife.

But the best laid plans don't always work out.

Its going to be a hell of a day!

ther amazing mythadventure from the masters of mayhem, the 2 Steves.

D0807713

Other books by Steve Barlow & Steve Skidmore

STONE ME! – Barn Owl Books

MIND THE DOOR! – Barn Owl Books

A TOUCH OF WIND! – Barn Owl Books

TALES OF THE DARK FOREST – HarperCollins
Goodknyght!
Whizzard!
Trollogy!
Knyghtmare!

LOST DIARIES – Harper Collins
The Lost Diary of Henry VIII's Executioner
The Lost Diary of Erik Bloodaxe, Viking Warrior
The Lost Diary of Shakespeare's Ghostwriter

VERNON BRIGHT – Puffin
Vernon Bright and the Magnetic Banana
Vernon Bright and Frankenstein's Hamster
Vernon Bright and the Faster-Than-Light Show
Vernon Bright and the End of the World

STAR BORES – HarperCollins

THE DOOMSDAY VIRUS – Barrington Stoke

FUNNY BUSINESS – Barrington Stoke

Steve Barlow & Steve Skidmore

DON'T LOOK BACK!

Illustrated by Tony Ross

BARN OWL BOOKS

First published in 2006 by Barn Owl Books
157 Fortis Green Road, London N10 3LX
Barn Owl Books are distributed by Frances Lincoln,
4 Torriano Mews, Torriano Avenue, London NW5 2RZ

ISBN 978-1-9030-1557-5

All rights reserved

Text copyright © 2006 Steve Barlow & Steve Skidmore
Illustrations copyright 2006 Tony Ross
Designed and typeset by Douglas Martin Associates
Printed and bound by Cox & Wyman Ltd, Reading

LLYFRGELLOEDD SIR DDINBYCH	
C46 0000 0443 321	
HJ	17-Sep-2009
JF	£4.99
PR	

Contents

Chapter One

EVERY PICTURE TELLS A STORY

"Hey! They've got no clothes on!" Well'ard Wally's gleeful voice rang out down the long, hushed art gallery. "Look at that one, sir! She's like my sister's teddy. She's a little bare."

Mr Latimer gave a long-suffering sigh. "Walter, in classical art it is usual to show the human form in its natural state . . ."

"And look at that naked bloke over there." Well'ard pointed. "He's got a great big . . ."

"Walter!" Mr Latimer's voice had a warning ring to it.

". . . bow and arrow," concluded Well'ard. Perce jabbed an elbow fiercely into his ribs.

"That's a cherub," said Eddie Johnson, who was listening avidly to the gallery audio guide that Mr Latimer had given out for his pupils' instruction. "You can tell because it's small and fat and it's got wings."

"Hey up, Cherub!" Well'ard waved at the pudgy archer.

"Look at his cheeks," said Claire Greene. "They're ever so pink."

Well'ard grinned. "I bet your cheeks would be pink if you went flying around in the . . ."

"*Walter!*"

"What, sir?" Well'ard's face wore an expression of angelic innocence that wasn't fooling anybody. There were furtive grins from several members of the group. Well'ard, stocky, untidy and impudent, was the class nutcase, and baiting teachers was his speciality. He called himself Well'ard because he reckoned he was well hard. If kids called him 'Walter', he would hit them until they agreed that 'Well'ard' was an appropriate nickname.

Mr Latimer's eyes closed momentarily, as though in pain. "I should be *grateful*, Walter . . ." (somehow, he managed to make it clear that by 'grateful' he meant, 'I shall restrain myself from flaying you alive – probably') ". . . if you would keep your idiotic observations to yourself. The rest of us have come on this school trip to the National Gallery to appreciate Art. We will now go and look at some old masters."

"But you're an old master sir," piped up Well'ard.

"We can look at you any time."

"Walter – I shall not tell you again." Mr Latimer turned on his heel and swept grandly down the gallery. His pupils shuffled unhappily behind him.

"Will you knock it off?" Perce hissed in Well'ard's ear.

"Knock what off?"

"Cheeking Latimer. This trip is boring enough when he's in a good mood."

"Well, I meantersay," grumbled Well'ard, "here we are in London, and what are we doin'? Bein' dragged round the National Rotten Gallery, lookin' at loads of pictures o' bowls o' fruit and cows in fields and Mad Donnas and stuff . . ."

"Mad Donnas?" Perce was baffled.

"You know – Mary and the baby Jesus . . ."

"Madonnas," prompted Eddie Johnson, who knew about these things. Eddie was as neat as Well'ard was scruffy, and had an insatiable thirst for knowledge – to the extent that he even claimed to enjoy school. In addition to being crazy, Eddie was accident-prone. Perce reckoned that if anyone dropped a piano from a great height, Eddie would be bound to be standing right underneath it –

with a dog widdling on his trouser leg.

"Whatever," said Well'ard dismissively. "There's all sorts of interestin' things we could be doin' instead! They got this dungeon place where you can see all the tortures they used to do with thumbscrews and red-hot pokers and stuff, sweet! I wouldn't mind seein' that. But here we are wastin' our time lookin' at mouldy old paintings."

Perce was forced to agree. The trouble with school trips was, when you were in school you'd dream of being on a school trip – but when the trip was like this one, you often wished you were back at school.

Well'ard took out the earphones for his MP3 player, and rammed them into his ears. Seconds later a rhythmic scratching noise indicated that, whatever Well'ard was listening to, it wasn't the gallery's audio guide.

Andy, who was walking in front of Perce, stopped so suddenly that she walked straight into him. Ruddy-faced, and with brown hair gelled so that it constantly stood to attention, Andy was Perce's best friend – which, naturally, meant that he came in for more of her spiky temper and barbed comments than anyone else.

But as Perce drew breath to tell Andy off for not looking where she was going, he pointed at a picture of a woman's head, with furious, staring eyes and snakes instead of hair. "Hey, Perce – remind you of anyone?"

Perce gazed at the face of Medusa the Gorgon, and shuddered. When she had first spotted the 'Scenes from Greek Myths' exhibition, it had seemed a good idea to persuade Mr Latimer to take them in to see it.

Mr Latimer had looked uncomfortable. "Priscilla," he said to Perce, (who grimaced: she hated anyone to use her real name), "in view of our past . . . er . . . experiences with characters from Greek legend, don't you think that might be tempting fate?"

"But, sir," Perce had said in her sweetest and most reasonable voice, "it'll be good for our education! And anyway," she went on blandly, "it's bad luck to be superstitious." Mr Latimer had given in and Perce had congratulated herself. She thought at the time that she'd been pretty clever. Now, she wasn't so sure.

It had been something of a shock when Andy

and Perce had discovered that they were distantly related to Andromeda, who had been tied to a rock and about to be chomped by a sea monster, and the hero Perseus, who had luckily come along to rescue her. At the time, Perseus claimed to have been carrying the head of Medusa the Gorgon – which was a bare-faced lie. Irritated by this self-promoting piece of codswallop Medusa had attempted to take revenge on the only surviving descendants of Perseus and Andromeda. She had appeared at Perce and Andy's school in the guise of a new supply teacher with a stare that gave a new meaning to the phrase 'hard look'.

Since then, Perce, Andy, Well'ard and Eddie had been plagued by a succession of heroes and monsters from Ancient Greece, who had done their best to make their lives interesting, uncomfortable and short. Most of these – along with a full supporting cast of flying cherubs, and misbehaving gods and goddesses – were pictured in the gallery where Perce and Andy now found themselves.

Letting the others flow round them like the tide round a rock, they stood stock still and turned on the spot. Over there, the Minotaur stalked its victims through the Labyrinth – while over *there*, the Sirens attempted to lure Odysseus and his sailors to their doom; and further along, Icarus, his damaged wings fluttering, fell endlessly to a watery death. Perce's lips twitched. At least, she hoped *that* had never really happened. She had liked Icarus . . .

The sound of a droning voice brought her back to the present. Perce looked down the gallery, and realised that Mr Latimer had brought the group to a halt in front of another exhibit. She and Andy hastened to join them.

"Now, this painting," Mr Latimer was gushing, "is a real treasure, and you are extremely lucky to have the chance of seeing it." About half the group, heads on one side, screwed up their eyes in an attempt to appreciate their good fortune: the rest continued to look bored.

Oblivious to their reaction, Mr Latimer waffled merrily on: "The picture is called *Orpheus Descends into the Underworld to Demand the Return of Eurydice.*"

Andy nudged Perce. "Yuri Deechy? She sounds Russian."

Perce grinned. "Perhaps that's why Orpheus went

rushin' into the Underworld to get her back."

"This magnificent work," Mr Latimer gushed, "was painted almost three hundred years ago by Jean Restout, and is on loan from the Louvre museum in Paris. It shows Hades, Lord of the Dead, and his wife Persephone, listening as Orpheus pleads for the return of his lost wife, Eurydice. Orpheus – who is, as you can see, singing and playing the lyre – was considered to be the greatest musician of the Ancient World."

Perce thought Orpheus – with his blond curls and slightly pudgy face – looked a bit of a wuss, but this probably wasn't a good time to say so.

"Why was Yuri Deechy lost, sir?" Eddie piped up.

"*Eurydice*," Mr Latimer corrected. "I'm glad you asked me that," he continued expansively as the rest of the group groaned. "The shepherd Aristaeus was dazzled by Eurydice's beauty. As she fled from him, she stepped on a snake. The poison of its bite proved fatal: but Orpheus decided to journey into the Underworld – to the land of the dead, from which no living man had ever returned – to bring her back."

Syreeta made a face. "Yeuch. Morbid."

"Did he get her back, sir?" persisted Eddie.

Mr Latimer shook his head. "Alas, no. Hades, Lord of the Dead, agreed to let her go, but only on condition that Orpheus should not look at Eurydice until they reached the living world. Unhappily, Eurydice was still lame from her wound, and could not keep up with Orpheus: so he glanced back to see that she was still following him, and she faded before his eyes, lost to him for ever."

"Awww." Claire's eyes had gone all misty. "That's dead romantic." Perce mimed putting her fingers down her throat.

Mr Latimer tore his eyes from the painting and cleared his throat. "Well, that concludes our visit. Our next stop will be the Natural History Museum." There were groans. "Here we will see an impressive collection of dinosaurs." The groans stopped; dinosaurs were cool. "So, when we leave here, we will turn left as we exit, then left again to walk northwards along Charing Cross Road to Leicester Square station where we will take a Piccadilly Line train in the direction of Heathrow Airport, and get off at South Kensington station." Mr Latimer whirled round and pointed an accusing finger at

Well'ard. "Where do we go next, Walter?"

Well'ard hastily snatched the earphones out of his ears. "Wot?"

Mr Latimer rolled his eyes. "I hope you realise I have had to write a separate risk-assessment file just for you. Put that thing away. You are quite capable of preventing my attempts to educate you from getting in the way of your ignorance without recourse to artificial aids."

Well'ard's eyes bulged as he tried to work this out. "Wot?"

"Never mind." Mr Latimer raised his voice to address the rest of the group. "Anyone who becomes detached from the group – *not that anyone will* – should rendezvous with the rest of us at South Kensington. And if in doubt, ask a policeman." He favoured Well'ard with another glare. "Walter, if *you* get lost – please *remain* lost for the sake of us all."

Chapter Two

ASSAULT AND BEEFEATER

"Now where are you off to?"

The group had left the gallery. Perce, Andy, Well'ard and Eddie were now standing on a corner, at the mercy of the winds that blew across Trafalgar Square.

Well'ard gave Perce a frosty look. "If it's any business of yours, I'm goin' over there . . ." He jerked his head towards a souvenir stall. "I wanna see if I can get somethin' for my mum."

Perce brushed strands of dark hair out of her eyes, then jammed her hands under her armpits to keep them warm and stamped her feet. "Well, hurry it up! It's freezing out here."

"All right, all right, don't get yer thermals in a twist."

As Well'ard browsed among the flags, pottery London buses and novelty teeshirts, Eddie remarked, "Funny seeing those pictures today. D'you think we'll get any more – er – *visitors* from Greek legends?"

Perce shuddered. "Let's hope not."

Andy nodded agreement. "They should have a Government Health Warning on those pictures: 'Tangling with mythological monsters can seriously damage your health'." He raised his voice. "Oh, come on, Well'ard! The others are nearly out of sight!"

Well'ard sauntered over, hands in pockets. "Nothin' there anyway. Load o'rubbish."

They set off to follow the school party, but had gone barely five paces when an angry voice bellowed menacingly above the traffic noise:

"'Ere! Where d'you think you're going with that?"

Well'ard kept his eyes rigidly forward. "Keep goin'," he muttered from the corner of his mouth, "and don't look back."

"'Ere! I'm talkin' to you!"

Ignoring Well'ard's instruction, Perce and the others turned to see the souvenir stall holder heading towards them, waving his arms aggressively. In the blink of an eye, he had Well'ard's shirt collar gripped tightly in his fist. "Give it back, sunshine," he growled.

"Hey, let go of him," said Perce. "That's assault."

"No it isn't." The stallholder fetched Well'ard a clip around the ear. "That's assault." His hand shot into Well'ard's coat pocket and brought out a glow-in-the-dark Beefeater snow globe. "And *that* is nicking."

"I was only lookin' at it!" Well'ard protested, rubbing his ear.

Perce rolled her eyes. "Oh, Well'ard . . ."

The stallholder stared hard at Well'ard. "Nice to look at, nice to hold, put it in your pocket and I consider it sold." He held out a large hand. "Payment is due for goods received; or rather, *taken*."

"I don't want it," said Well'ard, thrusting the globe towards its rightful owner.

"Too bad," the stallholder pointed out. "You've got it."

"I don't want to *pay* for it . . ." Well'ard corrected himself.

"Oh, I think you do," replied the stallholder. "Pay up, son. Or else . . ." He nodded across the street. The kids followed his gaze towards two policemen standing on the opposite pavement.

"Come on Well'ard, cough up," snapped Perce.

"Latimer will be going ballistic."

Scowling, Well'ard produced a crisp ten pound note from his pocket. The stallholder snatched it out of his hand. "That'll do nicely."

"Hey!" cried Well'ard. "I want change."

"You've got it," said the stallholder. "The ten pound note has changed into a glow-in-the-dark Beefeater snow globe."

Well'ard was outraged. "That's robbery!"

"No, taking stuff without paying is robbery." The stallholder turned to the others. "And I'm sure your friends want to buy a souvenir of this incident so they don't forget it and I *do* . . ." He nodded towards the policemen again.

Perce was quick to catch on. "But that's blackmail!"

"I prefer the term 'aggressive marketing'. Now come back to the stall and choose a wonderful memento of your day out!"

By the time Perce, Eddie and Andy had been forced to buy a selection of Tower Bridge mugs, sticks of London rock and amusing teeshirts from the souvenir stall, there was no sign of Mr Latimer and the rest of the class.

"Oh great," moaned Andy. "Now we're lost. Thanks Well'ard."

Well'ard remained silent, still stunned by his wealth reduction.

"Don't worry," said Eddie. "I heard what Latimer said. We can catch them up at Leicester Square tube station. I know the way. Trust me."

"Eddie, I'm never going to trust you again," said Perce. "We've just spent half an hour walking round in circles."

Andy patted a disconsolate Eddie on his shoulder. "I've not lost my trust in you . . ."

Eddie brightened. "Thanks, Andy."

" . . .'Cos I never had any trust in you in the first place!" Andy pointed at Nelson's Column. "Trafalgar Square! We're back exactly where we started!"

"So what do we do now?" said Well'ard.

"We could ask a policeman for directions," suggested Andy.

Well'ard's eyes narrowed. "No way! That's like fraternisin' with the enemy."

Perce sighed. "Well'ard, I swear you don't live

in the real world." She looked around. "Anyway, you're in luck and we're out of it. There's no policemen about."

"Typical," snorted Well'ard. "Always around when you don't want them to be and never around when you do . . ."

"This is all your fault, Well'ard," said Andy. "Why are you so stupid?"

"Years of practice," said Perce. Well'ard glowered. "Let's try again," she continued. "But this time we ignore Eddie and head off the opposite way." She trudged off with the others following in her wake.

As the kids made their way up Charing Cross Road, pushing their way through the crowds of tourists, Eddie sighed. "I knew today was going to be trouble," he said in a resigned voice. "My horoscope said I was going to meet a stranger and have a hell of a day."

Perce gave a snort of derision. "That's rubbish. 'Hell of a day' could mean 'hell of a *good* day' or 'hell of a *bad* day'. And how many strangers are you likely to meet in a city as big as London? Horoscopes are just like teachers . . ."

"Yeah," interrupted Well'ard, "'cos they're full o' rubbish."

"No," said Perce, "because the way they tell you what's going to happen, half the time you haven't got a clue what they're on about, and when it all goes wrong, it's not their fault for not explaining properly, it's your fault 'cos you didn't understand them. Like Latimer's directions," she added bitterly.

Eddie sniffed. "Well, I reckon the future is written in the stars."

"Well'ard's isn't," said Perce. "It's written in his probation officer's reports."

Well'ard scowled. "Your future will be in intensive care if you give me any more abuse . . . I'm as honest as the next man."

"Yeah," nodded Perce, "but only if the next man was Al Capone. Who just got us into trouble because he wanted a glow-in-the-dark Beefeater snow globe?"

Before Well'ard could issue any further threats, Andy gave a cry. "There it is! Leicester Square." He pointed towards a white building with the distinctive red and blue Underground symbol.

"I told you we'd find it," said Eddie.

"No thanks to you," complained Perce.

They made their way down the steps into the concourse. Perce looked around. "There's no sign of the others. They must have gone on ahead. Latimer'll be going spare."

"Serves him right for losing us . . ." muttered Well'ard.

Andy checked an Underground map. "Latimer said we needed to get to South Kensington. We take the Piccadilly Line . . ."

Brandishing the travel cards they'd been issued with at the beginning of their trip, they made their way through the ticket barriers and headed for the long escalator. As they travelled downwards cold air blew from the tunnels below and an eerie noise could be heard drifting upwards.

"Sounds like someone's in pain," said Well'ard.

"It's a busker," Perce told him. "The Underground's full of them. They play music and sing and people give them money."

"He's not going to earn much with singing like that," said Well'ard.

At the bottom of the escalator they found the

source of the singing. Before them stood a youth with a chubby face and curly blond hair. He was dressed in a sheepskin body-warmer and baggy trousers over which a white shirt, several times too large for him, hung loosely. He had a scarf spread out if front of him: coins dropped by appreciative passengers glinted here and there in its folds. He was playing a harp-like instrument that he held in one hand whilst plucking the strings with the other. The kids came to a halt and listened.

> *"Where shall I find Eurydice?*
> *Oh, how I miss my bay-bee!*
> *Eurydice! Gee, you're peachy!*
> *You're my dah-lin', please believe me!*
> *Want you in mah lovin' arms . . ."*

"Pants," said Well'ard. "Great, big, pink elasticated pants."

Perce disagreed. "It's not bad . . ."

Well'ard shook his head. "You're right . . . It's *worse* than bad, it's diabolical."

Disregarding the critical opinions of his audience the busker continued:

"Eurydice, please show meeee!
Eurydice, make me seeee!
Open the door to meeee!"

The singer suddenly stopped, held his instrument in front of him like a divining rod and closed his eyes. As Perce and the others stared, he moved down the corridor and turned round slowly twice before coming to an abrupt stop in front of an advertisement for an exhibition at the British Museum. The poster showed a Greek vase with the figure of a woman, her hands clasped together as though in a desperate plea. The busker gave a cry of joy. "Yes – the door is here! Thank you my love!" With a cry of triumph he ran headlong at the wall.

"Look out!" warned Perce. "Ooohh," she moaned as a loud crack echoed through the tunnel. As one, Perce, Eddie and Andy groaned and Well'ard gave a hoot of laughter. The busker slid bonelessly to the floor.

"Now, that is going to hurt," guffawed Well'ard. "What a nutter!"

Perce hurried over to pick up the prostrate busker. "Are you all right?" she asked.

The youth opened his eyes and looked up. "Eurydice? Is it you?"

"Guess again . . ." Perce hesitated as a terrible sense of foreboding swept through her. ". . . Eurydice? Did you say Eurydice?"

The youth nodded. "She is my beloved. I am searching for a hidden door."

Perce exchanged a worried glance with Andy. They knew all about hidden doors. She slowly turned to the others. "Remember the painting in the gallery?" she said. "The one about the Underworld?" She turned back to the busker and steeled herself.

"What's your name?"

"I am called Orpheus."

"I thought so," Perce's head dropped in resignation. "It's happening again. We're back in mythological trouble."

Chapter Three

ORPHEUS IN THE UNDERGROUND

Andy gave Perce a pitying look. "You're out of your tree!"

"He's right," said Well'ard, who never missed an opportunity to stir up trouble. "There's no way this bloke can be Orifice . . ."

"Orpheus!" retorted Perce.

"That's what I said!"

"Why can't he?"

"Because," said Eddie, joining in as Well'ard hesitated, "Orpheus was the greatest musician who ever lived, and he was given his harp by the god Apollo and his mum was the muse Calliope . . ."

Perce gawped at him. "How do you know all at?"

"It was on the audio guide. At the gallery."

"You akcherly *listened* to that thing?" Well'ard was disgusted.

"And the way he played and sang was so brilliant that it made even the rocks and trees dance.

The legend doesn't say anything about him busking down the Tube," Eddie continued. "And to be honest, I reckon if he was that good, he'd be able to come up with better lyrics than, '*Eurydice, you're so peachy*'!"

The busker who called himself Orpheus glared at Eddie. "You try finding new rhymes for 'Eurydice' after three thousand years!"

"Eddie, Orpheus – shut up, both of you!" Perce had become aware that the altercation was attracting a lot of attention, and holding up the Underground passengers who were trying to get to the platform. She took the busker by the sleeve; after a moment's resistance, during which he scooped up his scarf and money, he allowed her to lead him into a quieter side passage. The others followed.

Perce folded her arms and gave the busker a considering look. "Let's get this clear. Are you really telling us that you're over three thousand years old?"The busker nodded wearily. "Well, I must say, you're looking well on it. I wouldn't have put you a day over nineteen."

"You don't understand." The busker's voice was practically a wail. "Since I lost Eurydice, through my own fault, I am cursed to wander the earth in search of the door that will lead me down to the Underworld. Once I have found it, I shall go back to ask Hades, the Lord of the Dead, to release my beloved."

Perce said, thoughtfully, "So you've been singing about how much you miss this girl of yours for three thousand years?"

His eyes becoming moist, the busker nodded.

"Er – did it never occur to you – after, say, about a thousand years or so – that it was maybe time to let her go and move on?"

"You don't understand." The busker's whole body drooped. "It's my fault she's stuck in that dreadful place. I looked back." Tears rolled down his cheeks. "It was the one thing Hades told me not to do, but I just couldn't help it . . . she was taking so long . . ."

Andy nodded sympathetically. "I know what you mean – Perce is never ready when I call round – ow!" He rubbed his stinging arm. Perce glared at him, flexing her knuckles.

"But I know I can get her out. When I play my lyre, Hades will listen to me – he did before, he will again – if only I can find the door!" He stared at the poster of the Greek vase in despair.

"Wot's that thing you're playin'?" Well'ard was eyeing the harp-like instrument that the busker held as though it were a precious relic. "I've never seen nothin' like it before."

"A lyre."

"Who are you callin' a liar?" Well'ard bristled. "I'm tellin' the truth! I really haven't never seen one like it before . . ."

"That's the name of the instrument," Eddie told him.

"Oh, right." Well'ard pointed at it. "Can I have a go?"

The busker gave Well'ard a horrified look and clutched the lyre protectively to his chest. Mutely, he shook his head.

"Oh, go on," wheedled Well'ard, "I won't break it."

Perce gave him a scornful look. "Leave it out, Well'ard. You can't play it. You wouldn't even know which end to blow."

"I bet I could," insisted Well'ard. "I can play guitar."

Andy guffawed. "You? No way!"

"I've got hidden talents," protested Well'ard.

Perce nodded. "So well hidden, no one's ever discovered them." She turned back to the busker. "All right. Let's say that you're really who you say you are. Let's say you really are Orpheus, and you're still looking for Eurydice. What makes you think there's a door to the Underworld down here?"

"I don't know," Orpheus admitted. "I can never be sure. All I know is that when I do find the entrance, it will be somewhere underground. I just go to any place in the world where there are caves, cellars, catacombs, sewers . . ." Eddie wrinkled his nose in disgust ". . . underground railways like this - and I look." He sniffed unhappily. "I'll probably just keep on looking for ever . . ."

"Maybe not." Perce exchanged a look with Andy, who shrugged. "The thing is," Perce went on, "we seem to be pretty good at finding doors into your mythological world – whether we want to or not."

Orpheus looked puzzled. "I don't understand."

Perce took a deep breath. "Well, first there was Medusa . . ." She told Orpheus of their previous encounters with the creatures of myth. Andy and

34

Eddie put the occasional word in by way of explanation. Well'ard stood eyeing the lyre with a crafty gleam in his eye.

By the time Perce had finished her recital, Orpheus was looking quite excited. "So you think," he said eagerly, "that all of us together might succeed in opening the door where I, alone, have failed?"

Perce was beginning to regret her rash offer. "Well – yeah, I suppose so – but if we do that, how do we know what would come through?"

Eddie nodded solemnly. "It might be a monster – Polyphemus, the Cyclops, or the chimera, or the hydra – or the Symphalian birds, with wings, beaks and claws of iron that kill people by bombarding them with poisonous poo . . . I don't want some manky metal birds dropping deadly do-do on my–"

"Shut up, Eddie!" Perce shuddered. "You've made your point."

Orpheus waved away these objections, "Please you must try! Have you any idea what it's like, searching for thirty centuries, never at rest, beset by guilt, tormented . . ."

"All right, all right!" Perce bit her lip in thought. "Maybe if we spread out and check the adverts, one of the posters might be a fake – or something."

She moved away down the passage and began to run her fingers along edges of the posters. Andy watched her for a few moments, then shrugged and followed suit. Orpheus, with an expression of mingled hope and apprehension, carefully laid his precious lyre on the scarf, and joined them.

When he was sure that Perce, Andy and Orpheus were fully engaged in the search, Well'ard grinned at Eddie, raised a finger to his lips, and tiptoed over to the lyre. He picked it up and adopted a 'guitar hero' pose. Eddie giggled.

Holding the lyre at groin level, Well'ard mimed a complicated finger-pick, contorting his face into the expressions of anguish usually assumed by rock legends doing a solo break. Eddie held his ribs and writhed with silent laughter.

Right arm windmilling, and leaping about like a demented antelope, Well'ard mimed a succession of power chords. He misjudged the last one; his flailing arm caught the lyre, knocking it from his grasp. It plummeted to the hard concrete floor, and broke.

Perce and Andy spun round. Eddie and Well'ard

stood rooted to the spot, rigid with shock. Orpheus stared at the smashed instrument with a look of utmost horror and despair. "My lyre!" he howled. "Presented to me by the god Apollo! Three thousand years old!"

"Well," said Well'ard sheepishly, "at least it wasn't a new one."

Fingers twitching and face twisted into a vengeful snarl, Orpheus stepped forward. Well'ard and Eddie took one look at him, and bolted.

Chapter Four

GOING DOWN!

The sounds of the pursuit echoed down white-tiled, concrete-floored corridors as Eddie and Well'ard ducked and weaved around and between outraged commuters.

Perce was finding it hard to keep up with Orpheus. The enraged busker had scooped up the remains of his lyre and pounded off in pursuit of its destroyers, alternately weeping and bellowing blood-curdling threats, which had the effect of encouraging Eddie and Well'ard to develop an impressive turn of speed and maintain their lead.

Perce was getting a stitch. She slowed down, gasping for breath. Ahead of her, she saw Eddie and Well'ard duck under a chain with a sign on it reading 'NO ENTRY' with Orpheus at their heels and Andy not far behind. Forcing herself to follow them, Perce wrestled with the swaying chain for a moment, and then raced on. Skidding round a corner, she found herself in a white-tiled corridor. At the far end, Well'ard and Eddie were throwing themselves into what looked like a small cubicle. Accompanied by a high-pitched beeping, steel doors slid across behind them – just in the nick of time. Orpheus, still running at full pelt, slammed into the doors as they closed. He recoiled for a moment: then, as first Andy and then Perce came panting up to join him, he leapt forward to scrabble at the join between the doors and jab frantically at a button set in the wall to one side.

"That's no good," Perce told him. "They've gone down in the lift." She pointed towards a second set of closed steel doors. "We'll just have to wait for the other one."

Orpheus hammered on the doors. "By the golden arrows of Apollo, by the winged sandals of Hermes, by the trident of Poseidon – they shall pay!"

"You're right!" said Perce. Orpheus turned to stare at her as she continued, "They will pay." She pointed to the shattered lyre. "They'll pay for it to be repaired. That's a promise."

Orpheus held out the mangled instrument. Bits of the frame dangled, spinning, on the end of strings that gave out a faint, discordant jangling. "Repaired?" he wailed.

Perce grimaced. "I'm not saying it won't take some time . . ." She broke off as an urgent beeping announced the arrival of the other lift. "Come on. They're not going to get away with this."

Andy clutched at her shoulder. "Um – Perce . . ."

Perce shook him off and strode towards the lift. She planted a foot to stop the doors closing and turned to her companions. "Well?"

Orpheus gave a growl and swept into the lift. Andy dithered. "Er – Perce . . ."

"You're wasting time," snapped Perce. "Ready or not – going down!"

Andy dived through the doors as they closed. The lift lurched and began its descent. Perce folded her arms and glared at him. "Now – what was it you were trying to tell me?"

"Oh, nothing much," said Andy bitterly. "Just that there aren't any lifts on this station."

Perce spread her arms to indicate the metal walls surrounding them. "Newsflash, Andy! Yes there are. We're in one!"

"Yes, but we shouldn't be! When we were planning the trip, old Latimer made me check out disabled access on the Tube. Leicester Square doesn't have any lifts, only escalators. This lift shouldn't be here."

Perce shrugged. "Well, it is. You got it wrong, that's all. You were probably looking at the wrong station. It's an easy mistake to make, especially for a div with one brain cell . . ."

"I did not look at the wrong station! This lift doesn't exist!"

"Then how come we're in it?"

"Well, we were looking for a door, weren't we?" Andy gave Perce an apprehensive look. "What if we've found one?"

Perce caught her breath as this sank in. Orpheus gasped.

"So," said Andy in a strained voice, "where do you suppose this thing is taking us?"

The lights flickered. Without speaking, the lift's three occupants backed up against its walls, feeling them shudder with the vibration of its passage.

"Erm – doesn't it feel to you as if we've being going down an awfully long time?" said Perce in a voice that wasn't quite level.

Andy nodded.

"And wouldn't you say . . ." The wall quivered beneath Perce's fingers. "Wouldn't you say that we're going down rather *quickly?*"

The lights flickered again. Suddenly, impossibly, the lift was filled with a roaring, rushing wind that buffeted its occupants, forcing them to screw up their suddenly stinging eyes, whipping their hair into disarray, plucking at their clothing, driving the breath from their bodies.

Then, as instantly as it had started, the wind died away to leave an eerie calm. But now, the voices began – a chorus of wails, shrieks, and sobs followed by a burst of maniacal laughter that caused the hairs on the back of Perce's neck to stand on end. She, Orpheus and Andy stared at the trembling walls, then at each other.

More voices echoed around them: wailing voices, mournful voices; terrified, distraught, demented voices punctuated by screams and howls of despair. They seemed to come from all around the plummeting lift. The voices went on and on, lamenting, pleading for mercy, sobbing, weeping and groaning with loss, desolation, the death of hope. Perce realised that she was crying uncontrollably. Glancing at her companions, she saw that Andy and Orpheus, too, both had tears streaming from their eyes.

"Look!" Andy's strangled gasp and pointing finger drew her attention to the doors. A dull, red glow was visible in the join between them. As Perce watched, open-mouthed, the glow became brighter. She gasped, and snatched her hand away from the wall, which had suddenly become too hot to touch. The voices died away to be succeeded by a dull roaring and crackling. Now every seam of the walls was glowing as though the lift were surrounded by hungry flames, licking around it, searching for a way in. The air shimmered and danced in front of Perce, and sweat burst out on her brow. She glanced in horror at her companions. They were all about to be roasted like so many Christmas turkeys! Perce opened her mouth to scream . . .

. . . and the lift came to an abrupt halt. The glow vanished, the doors opened, and Perce, Andy and Orpheus staggered out to find themselves on a perfectly ordinary-looking Underground station. They were standing in a tunnel lined with white tiles, on a concrete platform. Before them, three steel rails ran along beneath the level of the platform and disappeared in dark tunnel mouths to their left and right.

Perce took several deep breaths. Then she gave what she intended to be a careless laugh, but which came out as an insane giggle. She turned an accusing look on Andy. "See what happens when you let your imagination run away with you? It's all right – here we are. Nothing to worry about."

Andy gaped. "You think so, do you? What about all that stuff in the lift? The wind . . . ?"

"Ventilation," said Perce airily.

Andy tried again. "Those creepy voices?"

"Echoes."

"The fiery glow?"

Perce shrugged. "Maybe they're installing a new lighting system."

Andy gritted his teeth. "All right, clever clogs – how do you account for *that*?"

Perce looked in the direction of Andy's pointing finger and gave him a pitying look. "It's just an Underground sign, Andy. We're on an Underground station."

"Yes, but there's no station *name* on it!"

"Well, maybe it's being repainted." Perce rounded on Andy. "Will you pack it in? You're just trying to scare me, and it's not going to work."

"The Underworld." Orpheus stared around. "At last. I am back in the Underworld. After three thousand years."

"Oh, don't you start!" Perce stamped her foot. "The Under*ground*. We're not in the Underworld, we're in the Underground. And here comes a train."

The tracks hummed. Lights appeared in the tunnel to their left. Seconds later, a train burst from the tunnel and rattled into the station, slowing as it came. It jerked to a halt. The doors hissed open. Perce stepped forward – and realised that neither Andy nor Orpheus had moved. She spun round to face them. "Come on! Well'ard and Eddie must have caught an earlier train. They'll be miles away by now."

Mutely, Andy shook his head.

"I said, come on!" Grabbing Andy with one hand and Orpheus with the other, Perce hauled them onto the train. The doors hissed shut and, with another jerk and a flash of blue light, the train

began to move. Perce eyed Andy's ashen face with disdain. "What is the *matter* with you?"

Andy pulled himself together with an obvious effort. "Well, if you hadn't been so busy dragging people about, you might have noticed that this train has no destination board . . ."

Perce stared at him. "What?"

". . . and no passengers . . ."

Perce spun around, and registered for the first time that the carriage was empty. "*What?*"

". . . and no driver."

Perce's face had turned as pale as Andy's. She slumped into a seat.

Beyond the rattling windows, the brightly lit platform came to an end. The train roared into the tunnel.

Chapter Five

ESCALATING HORRORS

The train came to a halt. The doors hissed open. Perce, Andy and Orpheus remained in their seats for several minutes, but the train showed no signs of moving.

Andy got up and poked his head cautiously out to look up and down the deserted platform. Then he drew his head back. He turned to Perce and Orpheus. "Hear that?" he said.

"Hear what?" Perce shook her head irritably. "I can't hear anything."

"Exactly! There should be an announcement. You know . . ." Andy put on a robotic voice. "*'This station is Wotaflippin Circus. Change here for the Circle, Metropolitan and Washing Lines. Passengers in the rear carriage alight from the front and mind the gap between your socks and trousers.'*"

Perce shrugged. Orpheus stepped cautiously onto the station platform, as though testing the feature-less concrete surface for quicksand or landmines.

Perce stood up. "Well," she said briskly, "there's no point sitting around here all day." She marched out of the carriage. Shaking his head, Andy followed.

Immediately, the doors slammed shut and the train departed.

Perce watched it go. "See? I knew we should have waited. Why are men so impatient?"

Andy opened his mouth to protest – and shut it again without speaking. Perce just wanted an argument because that was better than having to admit she was scared and didn't know what to do next. He looked around. "There's a station sign over there," he pointed out. "It says, 'Highgate'."

Perce dragged a crumpled map of the Underground from her pocket and opened it. "Highgate, Highgate . . ." she muttered. Then she gave a crow of triumph. "There it is! Highgate! See? I told you there was nothing wrong." She tapped a point on the map. "Here we are – Highgate, ten stops up from Leicester Square on the Northern Line."

"But we only travelled one stop to get here," Andy pointed out, "and we were supposed to be on the Piccadilly Line."

"Details, details." Perce's good humour was restored. "Both lines go through Leicester Square. We must have crossed from one to the other when Orpheus was chasing Well'ard and Eddie . . ." She broke off as something further down the platform caught her attention. "Speaking of which . . ."

She pointed. Halfway along the platform an arrow glowed, presumably showing the way out. From the side tunnel beneath it, two tousled heads and two pairs of worried eyes were peering in her direction.

Perce raised her voice. "You two! Come here!"

She heard a faint, "Oo-er!" and the heads vanished.

"There they are!" Perce turned to where Orpheus had been standing – and gawped. "Where'd he go?" Andy shrugged.

There was a sudden commotion from the spot where Eddie and Well'ard had first appeared. A few moments later, they came back into view; Orpheus was carrying Eddie in a fireman's lift and dragging Well'ard along by his ear. "He must have sneaked through another tunnel and come up behind them," said Andy.

"Oooowww!" howled Well'ard. "GBH! GBH! Unreasonable force! Police brutality! Leggo, you're hurting."

Orpheus halted in front of Perce and Andy. He released Well'ard, who stood poised for flight, giving him dark looks. Then he deposited Eddie on the platform.

"Are you going to beat them to a pulp?" asked Perce brightly. "Can I watch? I'll hold your coat for you, if you like."

Orpheus shook his head. "This is no time to quarrel among ourselves. Fate has thrown us together in this place. You do not know your peril." He looked around. "Whatever you may think, I feel in my bones that my wanderings are finally over. This is the Underworld."

Perce rolled her eyes.

"At last, I have returned, after three thousand years of searching." Orpheus's voice was grave. "Yet I cannot rejoice. Hades' realm is full of dangers to make the bravest quail . . ."

"To make the bravest quail what?" asked Eddie. "I hate to break it to you, but quails are very small birds, and they're not noted for being brave, so if you're counting on one of them to help you, I think you may be in for a bit of a disappointment . . ."

"To make the *bravest* quail," repeated Orpheus cuttingly. "I must attempt to rescue Eurydice; but to attempt is not to succeed. We must make our way to Hades' palace – but many dangers lie before us. We will need all our skill, wit and cunning to survive."

"Skill, wit and cunning, eh?" Perce gave a wolfish grin. "Eddie, Well'ard, you're dead."

"Do not make light of our situation," snapped Orpheus.

Perce was suddenly fed up with Orpheus's prophecies of doom. "Oh, shut up! We're in the Underground – all we have to do is go through to the other platform and get a train back the way we came . . ."

"There isn't another platform," said Well'ard glumly. "We've been looking for it ever since we got here. There's only this one."

Perce gave an impatient sigh. "All right, we'll go up to the street and get a bus. There are bound to be buses."

"Just one slight problem," said Eddie in a colourless voice.

Perce waited for a moment. "*Yes?*" she prompted.

"There's no lift," said Eddie, "and only one escalator."

"How many escalators do you *need?*"

"The point is," Eddie said, "it doesn't go up."
Orpheus nodded as if his worst fears had been realised.

Perce groaned. "So where *does* it go? As if I didn't already know the answer."

Eddie pointed at his feet. "Down."

They stood at the top of the escalator. The slatted floor formed itself into steps before them, which rumbled endlessly down into a sloping tunnel, to vanish, beyond the range of the lights, into abysmal darkness.

Eddie cleared his throat nervously. "Tell you what, let's go back to the platform and wait for another train."

Orpheus shook his head. "There will not be another train. We are in the Underworld. The only way is onwards."

Eddie groaned. "You know, I had a nasty feeling you were going to say something like that."

Orpheus stepped onto the moving stairway. After a moment's hesitation, Andy followed suit. Perce gave a sigh and followed. There was a brief scuffle behind her as Well'ard and Eddie fought not to be the last in line.

They slid down into the darkness. Andy jerked his head towards the walls. "Check out the adverts." Perce read the framed posters as they went past.

Instead of the normal glossy posters for films, shows, exhibitions and mobile phone companies, there were increasingly depressing slogans in gloomy gothic lettering:

Welcome to the undiscovered country from whose bourn no traveller returns
The way to Hades is paved with good intentions
Repent, for the end is nigh!
Turn back, brief mortals, before it is too late

And then a series of frames each bearing a single word, which read:

Abandon
Hope
All
Ye
Who
Enter
####### Here

After the last of these, the light faded. Gradually it was replaced by a sourceless red glow. The tunnel around them had changed from white tile to naked rock. And now, pictures began to appear on the walls. Behind Perce, Eddie whimpered.

The pictures showed terrible creatures: men and women with the heads of animals, birds and insects; human heads on the bodies of rats, spiders and scorpions. Grotesque, goat-horned satyrs rode on pigs, flying fish and beasts out of nightmare. Giants loomed out of the darkness, mad-eyed, their gnarled, clutching hands reaching out to rend and tear . . .

"You can't scare me!" Well'ard yelled defiantly. "You should see my mum and dad!" The things howled and gibbered.

"Don't provoke them," hissed Perce.

"Why not? They're provoking *me!*"

Andy gave Perce a hard-eyed stare. "So, how do you explain this? An experimental sound-and-light show to entertain passengers? Or are you finally going to admit that we really *are* in the Under-world?"

"Okay, okay." Perce grimaced. "Maybe – maybe breaking Orpheus's lyre was the . . . I dunno, the key, or the trigger, or whatever, that would let him back down here . . ."

"That would make sense," said Orpheus. He clenched his fists. "Hades might have arranged it so I could return only after breaking the one thing that might give me power over him. The old devil always did have a warped sense of humour."

Perce rounded on Well'ard and Eddie. "Well done! This is another fine mythological mess you've got us into!"

As she spoke, the light changed from fiery red to dismal blue. The bestial, prancing figures dis-appeared. The tunnel was coming to an end. The steps beneath their feet folded flat and disappeared under a slatted steel floor. One by one, they stepped off the escalator onto yet another station platform. A sign on the wall read, 'Embankment'.

But this time, there was no track running along the platform, and no tunnel wall beyond. Where the track should be was water – dead, black, all but motionless, lapping against the platform with a sound almost too faint to be heard.

From the darkness before them, a hollow, echoing voice intoned, "Welcome, rash travellers, to the realms of the dead . . ."

Chapter Six

FERRY INTERESTING

A faint glow appeared far out over the inky water. Perce and her companions watched as the light, bobbing gently, moved unhurriedly towards them. Before long, they could see that it came from a lantern, hanging from the high stern of a boat. A cowled figure stood beneath the light, its face invisible in the shadows of its deep hood. Bony wrists protruded from the sleeves of its robes: skeletal fingers gripped a single oar with which the figure propelled the boat across the calm water.

The prow of the boat bumped against the station platform. The boatman rested on his oar. From within the dark folds of the hood came a low, melancholy voice. "Well, well. Orpheus. Long time no see."

Orpheus gave the robed figure a brief nod. "Charon."

Well'ard nudged Perce. "*Sharon?* I could've sworn it was a feller in there."

Orpheus had heard the muttered comment.

"Charon is the ferryman who carries the souls of the dead into Hades' realm. He is here to take us across the River Acheron."

"I thought it was the River Styx," protested Eddie.

"A common mistake," said Charon. "There are five rivers in the land of the dead. The Styx lies further in. To reach Hades' palace, you must first cross the Acheron – the River of Woe."

"Nice name." Eddie drew back in alarm. "Thanks, but no, thanks. I get seasick looking at a goldfish bowl, and anyway I'm excused crossing rivers of death on account of not being dead . . ." He looked into the shadows beneath Charon's hood and added, in a quavering voice, "Yet."

The melancholy voice from within the hood said, "That can be arranged."

"Well, this has been a really interesting and novel experience, but you know what?" Eddie stuck his hands in his pockets in a ghastly display of nonchalance. "I've just remembered I have an appointment with the dentist, or to get my hair cut, something like that, so if you could just point me in the direction of the way out . . ."

"There is no way back," Charon intoned. "The

only way is onwards."

Eddie's shoulders slumped. "Terrific!"

"Oh, come on!" Perce stepped towards the boat; on the edge of the platform she turned to face the others. "All aboard!"

"Not so fast!" Charon was holding up a bony hand, palm outwards, gesturing Perce to stay where she was. Then the hand shot out, thumb rubbing against the first two fingers in a universal gesture. "Who will pay the ferryman?"

"Great!" said Andy to no one in particular. "It's not enough that this bloke wants to carry us off to the land of the dead – now he wants paying for it as well!"

Perce put on her most appealing smile. "Couldn't you just – take us to the other side?"

The hood shook from side to side. "Sorry, lady. No can do. Company policy. Lost souls, fine – they used to pay me with the pennies that were put over their eyes before they were buried, but that's a dying custom – Hah hah hah! Dying custom, get it?" He shook his head sadly. "They try all sorts these days. Old bus tickets. Air miles. And don't talk to me about loyalty cards . . ." Charon sighed.

"Sometimes I just let a few slip in on the back. But carry mortals without a fare?" The ferryman sucked in his breath. "Oh dear me, no. Couldn't do it. More than my job's worth."

Perce turned an enquiring glance on Orpheus, who held out the scarf containing the money he had made busking. Charon gave it a cursory glance. "One pound seventy-five and a car wash token — that's not going to get you very far."

"Told you he was rubbish," muttered Eddie.

Perce nudged Orpheus. "You've been here before — how do we get across?"

Orpheus shrugged unhappily. "Last time I was here I charmed Charon with my music . . ."

"Charmed?" spluttered the hooded figure. "Charmed, he says? I can think of another word for it! After a few minutes of his singing, I offered him a lift if he promised to stop!"

"In any case," Orpheus went on hurriedly, "I'm afraid . . ." He held up the remains of his broken lyre.

"Tut tut tut." Charon clicked his tongue. "Well, tough luck, chummy. Come back and see me when you're dead." He made as though to shove off.

"Wait!" Perce turned to the others. "We must have something he wants. More money?"

"Don't look at me!" protested Well'ard. "I'm skint."

"We all are," said Andy mournfully, "Thanks to Well'ard." Then he brightened. "We've got souvenirs of London," he said hopefully. "Tower Bridge mugs, sticks of London rock, teeshirts with funny slogans, a glow-in-the-dark Beefeater snow globe."

Charon's hood shook wearily from side to side. "Do me a favour."

Perce thought furiously for a moment. "So, you don't like music?"

Charon nodded eagerly. "Oh, yeah, 'course I do. If you were stuck down here with nobody but lost souls for company (and between you and me, they're a pretty miserable bunch – well, you can't blame 'em, stands to reason), you'd fancy a bit of music, wouldn't you? Cheers the place up, like."

Perce raised an eyebrow. "But if you like music, why didn't you want to listen to Orpheus singing?"

"Because I like music," said Charon pointedly.

Orpheus sniffed. "Everyone's a critic."

"Then I know how we can pay for our passage."

Perce swung round and pointed at the MP3 player that was poking out of Well'ard's top pocket. "Hand it over."

"No way!" Well'ard was outraged. "This cost a fortune. It's got six thousand songs on it."

"Well, that should see us across all right – or do you want to sit here for ever?"

Well'ard took a lot of persuading, but at long last, grudgingly, he handed the MP3 player over. Perce stepped into the boat and instructed Charon on how to fit the earphones and select a track. A tinny scratching noise came from the hood. Charon perked up immediately. "Hey, cool! Get in dudes, you've got yourselves a ride."

Carefully, the other four embarked. Perce, Andy and Eddie settled themselves onto the hard wooden seats and stared out apprehensively across the black waters of the River Acheron. Well'ard and Orpheus sulked.

Charon shoved the boat out and twisted the oar through the gurgling water. Before long, the station platform behind them had faded from view. The little boat was all alone on the calm, treacle-black surface of the river of the dead.

"I had that King Henry the Eighth in the back of my boat once," Charon said conversationally. "Great big fat lump he was – he nearly sank me. Oh yes, I've carried them all across here – Vlad the Impaler, Doctor Crippin, Rasputin the Mad Monk, Mrs Wiggins of Muswell Hill . . ."

"Mrs Wiggins of Muswell Hill?" Perce was nonplussed. "Why include her with all those monsters? What did she do?"

"Ooh, *her*!" Charon chuckled reminiscently. "She was the worst of the lot. Oh dear, oh dear, oh dear."

"But I've never heard of her!"

"That's because she never got caught." Perce thought about this as their guide rowed onwards, humming along to the music that only he could hear. The only sounds were the rhythmic swish of the oar blade and scratching noises from the earphones beneath Charon's hood. From time to time, the ferryman's voice would rise, joining in with the line of a chorus.

"*By the River of Acheron*," he warbled, "*which I row down . . .*"

Orpheus winced. "And he has the nerve to criticise *my* singing . . ." He lapsed into gloomy silence.

After a voyage that seemed endless, Perce realised that a light was growing in the distance. As they approached it, she saw that they were heading for what looked like another Tube station platform. Before long, the Underground signs along the platform bearing the name of the station became visible.

Andy read them. "Barking," he said softly.

The boat bumped gently against the platform. Perce scrambled out, followed by the others. She led the way along the platform to the exit, rounded the corner into a side-tunnel – and stopped.

Across the tunnel lay the body of a gigantic dog. It was lying with its back towards them, its flank rising and falling as it snored.

Perce tried to breathe more quietly. "Now what do we do?"

"Climb over it?" hissed Andy.

Perce would have made a cutting remark about the stupidity of that suggestion, but at that moment the snoring stopped and a fierce-looking canine head rose to stare at them with glowing, unfriendly eyes.

"Nice doggy," said Perce without conviction.

Another head appeared, growling. Perce gulped. "Er . . . Nice doggy."

A third head rose up, its lips pulled back in a snarl. "Nice . . . doggy," wavered Perce, backing into the others. "Andy, are there three dogs here?"

Andy gulped. "Nope. One dog, three heads."

Orpheus's voice was a wail. "Cerberus!"

The great beast rolled over and sprang to its feet. Stiff-legged, six eyes glaring, six nostrils flaring and a hundred and twenty-six teeth bared in three savage snarls, the monstrous hound stalked towards Perce and her helpless companions.

Chapter Seven

HEADBANGER

Standing before the quaking group, the black hell-hound threw back its heads and barked, bayed and howled like a thing possessed.

"Don't worry," Andy bravely reassured the others. "A barking dog never bites – at least, not while it's barking."

"But only *one* of its heads is barking," Eddie pointed out.

Andy gulped. "Then two of us are in big trouble!"

As if in response to Andy's observation, Cerberus fell silent.

"Correction," moaned Andy, "*three* of us are in big trouble. And even the other two probably shouldn't make any long-term plans . . ."

Cerberus padded menacingly towards the intruders, its slavering muzzles set in a three-pack of threat with an Added Free Bonus Sample of terror.

"Don't move!" ordered Orpheus.

"Guess what?" said Perce standing stock-still. "I wasn't going to."

"It will not attack us," said Orpheus, "unless we try to pass by."

"Hey," said Perce, "I vote we don't try to pass by. Those in favour?" Four hands shot up. "Those against? Motion carried!"

Well'ard tugged at Orpheus's sleeve. "What is that thing, Orifice?"

"That's *Orpheus*," snapped Perce.

"Wot, the dog's called Orifice as well? That's a bit of a coincidence!"

"The *dog*," replied Orpheus, "is called Cerberus. The demon of the pit: the guardian hound of hell. Its job is to stop the living getting into the Underworld and to make sure the dead don't get out."

"Sir Boris, eh?" Well'ard was impressed. "That's some guard dog; I reckon he'd have our Doberman for breakfast."

The gatekeeper of the Underworld continued to pad back and forward, barring the way to the tunnel opening.

"He is the child of Echidna and Typhon," continued Orpheus. "They were hideous monsters.

71

Their children were many and gruesome."

"They sound like Well'ard's mum and dad," said Perce.

Well'ard made a move towards her, but came to a sudden halt as Cerberus gave a warning growl. "If Sir Boris wasn't there," Well'ard told Perce, "you'd be in trouble."

"The brothers and sisters of Cerberus," Orpheus continued, "include the Nemean lion and the Hydra who fought Heracles, and the Sphinx."

Andy whistled. "Some family. I bet they've had more ASBOs than Well'ard . . ."

"I didn't deserve 'em," protested Well'ard. "I was hounded by the police."

"And now, we're being hounded by Rover here." Perce thought furiously. "We need to find a way out of this mess." She looked back across the black water for an escape. There was none: Charon had long disappeared. Perce frowned, wondering what to do. "We can't go back and we can't stay here, we have to get past that thing . . ."

"He will not rest until we have gone," said Orpheus. "To have come so far and be thwarted by a mere dog. . ." he tailed off mournfully.

"Hang on," said Eddie. "Didn't you get past Cerberus when you were down here last time?"

Orpheus nodded.

"Then why didn't you say so?" snapped Perce, "instead of making us stand here like we're playing a game of musical statues? How did you do it?"

"I sang him to sleep."

"I can believe that," said Well'ard. "He was probably bored out of his minds."

"So why don't you sing to him now?" said Perce.

Orpheus shook his head. "Before, I had my lyre." He stared hard at Well'ard. "Which is now broken, thanks to you."

"Hey, I've suffered as well," said Well'ard bitterly. "I had to give my MP3 to Sharon. We could have used that."

"It wouldn't have been much good anyway." Eddie gestured towards Cerberus. "One set of earphones. Three heads. That's only two-thirds of a earphone per head. It'd never work."

Perce gave Well'ard a smile. Her voice was sickly sweet. "Well'ard . . . you're tough aren't you?"

Well'ard eyed Perce suspiciously. "Of course . . ."

"And brave?"

73

"Yeah . . ." answered Well'ard, warily.

"Then you're the one who should get over there and sort that dog out."

"Why me?" demanded Well'ard.

"'Cos you're tough and you've got a Doberman."

"Yeah, vicious great bad-tempered brute. I never go near it."

"But you keep telling us you don't know the meaning of the word 'fear'."

"I don't the meaning of a lot of words." Well'ard gestured towards Cerberus. "But I'm not messing with that thing."

Eddie gave a loud laugh that turned into an embarrassed cough as Perce rounded on him. "If you think it's so funny, why don't you get over there and sort it out?"

"Me?" said Eddie. "How stupid do you think I am?"

"Put it this way," said Perce, "you couldn't hit sand if you fell off a camel. Just go over to the nice doggie and give it a friendly pat . . ."

"Pat it?" squeaked Eddie. "How do you know it won't bite?"

"I don't," said Perce reasonably. "That's why I

want you to pat it . . ."

"No way."

Perce sighed. "We must be able to think of something. Five heads are better than three."

"We're caught between a rock and a hard place!" moaned Andy. "By the time Cerberus has finished with us, we'll end up in the River Styx."

"Acheron," said Orpheus, "not the Styx . . ."

"Rocks! Styx!" Eddie cried out. "That's brilliant!"

Andy looked puzzled. "What is?"

"What you said." Eddie rummaged in his bag for a couple of seconds before producing the two sticks of pink rock he'd been forced to buy from the souvenir stall in Trafalgar Square.

"Eddie!" snapped Perce. "This is no time for eating sweeties!"

Eddie grinned. "That's what you might think I'm thinking of doing, but you'd be wrong to think that that's what I'm thinking." He crawled over to Perce and whispered in her ear.

"Amazing!" said Perce when Eddie had finished. Eddie beamed. "What, the plan?"

"No – that someone as nutty as you could come up with it."

Eddie scowled.

"Hand it over then."

Eddie passed Perce one of the sticks of rock. Taking the bright pink sweet, she edged away from Eddie until she was against the tunnel wall. Meanwhile Eddie had moved to the opposite side of the tunnel. Andy, Well'ard and Orpheus looked on bemused. Cerberus stood snarling, one set of eyes trained on Eddie, another on Perce whilst its middle head viewed the others.

Eddie waved at Cerberus. "Good boy," he called. "Who's a good boy?"

All of Cerberus's six eyes looked quizzically at Eddie. In all of its existence, the feared Demon of the Pit had never been called a 'good boy'.

Perce held out a flat hand. "Sit!" she ordered. "That's a good boy – sit!"

Some primeval instinct stirred inside the creature's three minds. With a joyful wag of its tail, Cerberus plonked its demonic bottom on the ground, its three tongues lolling from its slobbering mouths.

This was the decisive moment. Perce exchanged glances with Eddie. "On the count of three," she said. "One . . . two . . . three . . ."

With a cry of "Fetch!" Eddie and Perce both threw their sticks of rock. The sticks spun through the air, passing in front of Cerberus's heads. Again, primeval doggy instinct took over: Cerberus leapt up, its mouths wide open. Its right head lunged at Eddie's stick, whilst its left was intent on catching Perce's. With a bone-splitting noise, the hound's left head and right head smacked into its middle head.

CRACK!

The companions winced.

"Heads," said Perce, "you lose."

Cerberus gave a puzzled yowl: "Arroorrr?" Then its six eyes rolled into the back of its heads and the doorkeeper to the Underworld crashed unconscious to the ground.

"I wonder if it's seeing stars or little birdies," pondered Eddie.

"This isn't the time to be bothered about that," snapped Perce, "This is the time to be bothered about running away before it wakes up."

The companions made their way cautiously past the senseless body of Cerberus. As they hurried

down the tunnel, Orpheus patted Eddie on the shoulder. "You did well," he said.

Andy and Well'ard nodded their approval. Even Perce had to admit that Eddie had excelled himself. "Nice plan," she said, grudgingly.

Andy gasped. "Crikey, Eddie, you've just received a compliment from Perce. The Earth must have stopped moving!"

Perce glared at Andy. "Down here, we wouldn't know if it had. We need to get Eurydice back for Orpheus and find our way back out. So stop being sarky and move your butts!"

Chapter Eight

GHOST TRAIN

Before long, they emerged onto another platform. Beyond this lay not a tunnel wall, but a grey plain stretching out to an invisible horizon. A train was waiting with its doors open – a bigger, boxier train than the ones they had already taken. A sign on its side read *Deadlands Light Railway*.

With a shrug, Perce led the way on board. As soon as the travellers were inside the carriage, its doors closed and they were off once again.

The train clattered across a featureless landscape. Perce and the boys pressed their noses against the windows, trying to see as much as possible of the dismal realm through which they travelled.

The sky was grey, flat and leaden. On either side of the train spread a dreary expanse of grass, with clumps of spiky white flowers here and there. Shadowy figures wandered across the plain: they looked like ghosts, half-transparent. Some turned to look at the train, but gave no other reaction.

"The flowers are Asphodel," said Orpheus. "This is the Plain of Asphodel, where most of the souls of the Dead reside. They remember nothing of their lives on Earth. They feel no pain, no ambition, no joy, no sorrow." Perce shuddered.

But soon, the train was running through a valley, and the souls outside were showing more animation. They wailed, and wept, and tore at their insubstantial clothes. "The Vale of Mourning," sighed Orpheus, "where dwell those who took their own lives, or were consumed by unhappy love. Maybe Hades will decree that I should join them."

A glow in the distance grew brighter. Seconds later, the train was hurtling alongside a river. Its waters were ablaze with crackling flames.

"Phlegethon, the river of fire." Orpheus pointed. "Beyond it lies Tartarus, the deepest and darkest pit of this realm. The eternal prison of the giants, the titans, and all those who die with their sins unforgiven." Perce and the others blinked away from the fierce blaze.

Then they were crossing another plain, where an unending line of ghostly figures shuffled slowly onward between what looked like tape barriers, as if they were queuing for a theme-park ride. The line zig-zagged on and on into the endless distance. "The Plain of Judgement, where souls are condemned to Tartarus or . . ."

"Tell me," said Perce, interrupting Orpheus, "aren't there any *nice* places down here?"

"Oh, yes," said Orpheus unexpectedly. "The Elysian Fields, where the souls of those who led worthy lives dwell in bliss. But we won't be going there."

"Typical," muttered Perce. "Just like a school trip. You always miss out on the good bits . . ."

The train came to a bone-jarring halt. With a loud whoosh, the doors flicked open. A robotic voice intoned, "This station is Barbican. Alight here for the palace of Hades. The next station on this line is Elysian Fields."

"We are here!" said Orpheus, stepping out of the carriage. "Barbican – the gateway to Hades' palace."

"Correct," snapped a voice from behind them. "And where the Hades have you been?"

The speaker was a furious-looking girl. She planted her fists on her hips and glared at Orpheus. "So, you've finally come back! What time do you call this? How long have you been out?"

"Erm . . ." Orpheus looked shamefaced. "Three thousand years, give or take a century."

Eurydice snorted. "Yes, off with the boys again I suppose – Jason and his cronies, the argonuts or whatever you called yourselves. Wandering all over the place causing trouble, looking for some stupid golden egg . . ."

"Fleece," corrected Orpheus. "It was a golden fleece."

"I don't care if it was a fur coat with matching accessories! You'd rather spend time with Jason than with me – I don't know why you didn't marry him!"

Perce would normally have taken the girl's side in an argument of this sort, but seeing Orpheus's woebegone expression, she couldn't help feeling that Eurydice was being a bit hard on him. "Go easy," she protested. "He's been looking for you for three thousand years!"

Eurydice gave her a look that would have curdled milk. "Who is this?"

"Her name is Perce," said Orpheus uneasily. "She is my companion . . ."

"I'm sure she is!" Eurydice gave a disdainful sniff. "Is she a goddess?"

Orpheus looked Perce up and down, from straggly hair to scuffed shoes. "I don't think so," he said tactfully.

Eurydice raised her eyebrows and her nose simultaneously. "Then how does she happen to be with you?"

Perce was nettled. "We just *happened* to meet your husband while he was looking for you," she said, indicating Andy, Well'ard and Eddie who were wisely staying out of the argument. "We just *happened* to help him find the way back down here after three thousand years. So if you could *happen* to stop making leery remarks, that would be very nice, thank you so much."

Orpheus said quickly, "Dearest, without these four, I might never have found you. They speak truly – I have been searching for thirty centuries."

"And whose fault is that?" Eurydice's face twisted into a sneer as she mimicked her husband's voice. "*Come along dear, do keep up, don't drag your feet, you'd be late for your own funeral games* . . . you just had to look back, didn't you?"

"Let's not dwell on the past," said Orpheus loudly, "I'm here now. I have come to beg Hades once more for your release."

"Oh, goodie!" If Eurydice was pleased, she hid it well. "And how, pray, were you planning to do that? Have you brought him presents of great worth? Rich oils and rare spices? Gold and precious stones? Things like that?"

"I thought," said Orpheus, "that I would charm him with the sound of my voice and my playing upon the lyre . . ."

"Gosh, how original!" Eurydice's voice dripped sarcasm.

"Well, it worked last time," said Orpheus defensively. "Only . . ." Shamefaced, he held out the smashed lyre for his wife's inspection.

"Better and better!" said Eurydice bitterly. "Well, come on, we'd better go and see Hades. I could do with a good laugh." She turned and stalked away. Orpheus mooched glumly after her. The others exchanged glances, and followed.

. Before long, a rocky hillside rose out of the plain. As they drew near, Perce saw two great bronze doors set into the rock. An old-fashioned wrought-

iron bell-pull hung beside the door. A notice beneath it said, 'NO JUNK MAIL'.

Eurydice tugged at the pull. Somewhere far away, a bell tinkled. Moments later, the doors opened to reveal a long corridor flanked with rough-hewn stone pillars and lit by flickering torches. Without hesitation, Eurydice strode inside. Orpheus trailed after her. With considerably more reluctance, Perce and the boys followed.

"Any second now," said Perce, "that door is going to go . . ."

CLANG!

"Told you." Perce glanced back over her shoulder at the doors that had slammed closed behind them, trapping them in the heart of Hades' realm.

Chapter Nine

HELLRAISERS

At length, the corridor opened out into a stone-walled room with a vaulted ceiling and a flagstone floor. Iron doors stood at the other end of the room. Here and there hung tapestries showing scenes from the Underworld through which they had recently passed.

"What's that satyr doing with that great long spear?" Eddie peered closer at the tapestry, and winced. "Oooooh. That's not nice."

"Oh, hello! Orpheus, isn't it? You're *quite* a stranger." In the middle of the room, Orpheus and Eurydice were being greeted by a small, fussy-looking woman with grey hair. She was wearing a pleated woollen skirt, a pink jumper, a pearl necklace and sensible flat-soled shoes. On a table behind her stood a vase of flowers, which she had evidently been arranging. Orpheus was pleading with her in a low voice.

The fussy little woman shook her head indecisively. "Well, my dears, you can ask him, but I really don't know what he'll say. He's been *very difficult* lately." She moved a couple of flowers around in a dispirited sort of way. "Oh dear – they're wilting already." She sighed. They always do, down here, no matter how hard I try. It's just too dark for the poor things . . . She broke off as she caught sight of Perce. "But who's this?" Her gaze took in Andy, Well'ard and Eddie. "Mortals, if I'm not mistaken. How delightful. We get so few visitors down here. How are you, my dear?"

Perce hesitated, unsure of what to say.

The fussy woman clicked her tongue. "Where are my manners? I'm Persephone, wife of Hades." She held out a wrinkled hand.

Perce shook it awkwardly. "Er – pleased to meet you – Ma'am," she said, hoping that this was the correct way to address the Queen of the Dead. "I'm Perce, this is Andy . . . Well'ard . . . Eddie – we're just trying to help Orpheus get Eurydice back . . ."

Persephone fluttered her hands helplessly. "I'd like to help you, my dears, I really would . . ."

Orpheus fell to his knees. "Oh, dread Queen of Hades, I beg you: persuade your husband to let

89

me take my darling Eurydice back to the upper world." His darling Eurydice glared at him and folded her arms.

Perspehone dithered. "Oh, dear . . . I don't mind, really; I should miss dear Eurydice of course . . ." She absent-mindedly patted Eurydice's hand. "Would you like to go, my dear?"

"Oh, I don't know," said Eurydice sarcastically. "It's been such a short visit, only three thousand years, goodness, doesn't time fly when you're having fun!"

Perce began to think that if anyone deserved an eternity in the Underworld, it was Eurydice.

"Well, we can but try." Persephone sighed. "Let's hope he's in a good mood . . ."

She was interrupted by a blare of trumpets, a crash of thunder, a mighty rushing wind; the doors at the far end of the room were flung open and a terrible apparition appeared.

Well'ard gawped. "Oh, hell," he said.

The newcomer gave Well'ard an unfriendly look and wiped his nose with the back of his hand. "That's 'Hades' to you," he growled.

Perce, Andy, Well'ard and Eddie stared at the

unlikely figure standing before them: the Lord of the Underworld, son of the titan Cronus, brother of Zeus and Poseidon – the great god Hades. He was wearing wire-framed glasses, a threadbare Fair Isle sweater, baggy tweed trousers and carpet slippers.

"You're Hades?" said Perce in disbelieving tones.

Hades nodded. "The very same."

"*The* Hades?" persisted Perce.

The Lord of the Underworld scowled. "That's my name. Don't wear it out."

"You're – er – not really what I expected," admitted Perce, vaguely remembering the paintings in the National Gallery. "I thought you'd be more sort of Greek looking – sandals and a toga . . ."

"Shows how much you know," scoffed Hades. "Romans wore togas. Oh, I used to wear a Greek chiton, three thousand years ago – stupid thing! All right for Earth or Olympus, but down here in the Underworld, it's just not practical. No sun . . . and the wind whips right through you. I'm comfortable in a nice warm woolly jumper and slippers. Why not? It's not as if we ever go anywhere." Hades adjusted his spectacles to peer more closely at his visitors. "So, you know who I am. And if

I'm not mistaken – which, being a god, I'm not –
you are Perce . . . and Andy . . . and Edward . . .
and Wallyhard . . ."

"It's *Well'ard!*"

"I daresay it is," said Hades vaguely. "Don't wear
it out, will you?"

Perce grinned at the furious Well'ard. "Be fair,
you get everyone else's name wrong."

Hades glared at his remaining visitor. "Orpheus!
I thought I had a restraining order banning you
from coming down here."

Orpheus shuffled his feet. "Oh great Hades,
Immortal God of the Underworld, Son of Cronus,
brother of Zeus and Poseidon . . ."

"You want something don't you?" Hades shook
his head. "You can always tell when humans start
off like that – they want something."

Shamefaced, Orpheus nodded. "Yes," he mum-
bled, "I want my beloved Eurydice."

Hades shook his head. "I can't let her go, just
like that. Can't be done. What would people say?
'Silly old fool's going soft in the head – granting
requests without some kind of remuneration.' You

93

should have listened to me. What did I say? 'Don't look back,' I said, and what did you do?"

"He looked back," snapped Eurydice. "Left me down here for years, all because he couldn't follow a simple set of instructions!"

Orpheus held out his hands in supplication. "I'll do anything . . .!"

"Is that a fact?" Hades clicked his fingers. "You could sing a song! We like a good song, don't we Persephone?"

The Queen of the Dead nodded enthusiastically. "Oh yes, dear, you sang so beautifully last time. I've been on and on to Hades about getting you back here . . ."

"You certainly have," muttered Hades. "On and on and on . . ."

"So now if you sing to us again, I'm sure my hubby will let Eurydice go . . . won't you, dear?"

"I might," said Hades loftily.

Orpheus was crestfallen. He held out his battered lyre. "Sadly, my instrument is broken."

Persephone eyed the remains. "Oh, dear."

Hades' mouth twitched into a crafty grin. "Is it really? Gosh, there's a thing . . ."

The penny dropped for Perce. "You were right," she told Orpheus. She turned back to Hades. "You planned all this!" she accused. "You arranged it so that Orpheus couldn't find the door to get down here until he'd broken his lyre."

Hades nodded smugly. "Of course. Your friend was very clever last time, getting into the Underworld and past Cerberus and persuading me and the wife to let him go with this girl of his." He gave Orpheus a nasty look. "A suspicious person might say he conned us. But no hard feelings." The Lord of the Underworld folded his arms. "Let's see him do it again – *without* his precious lyre!"

Chapter Ten

HELL'S A-BOPPIN'

"Oh hubby," huffed Persephone. "I might have known this was one of your little games."

Hades took his glasses off and wiped them on the tail of his collarless shirt. "Just keeping myself amused."

Perce was furious. "This has all been just a game?"

Hades chuckled. "It's what we gods do best. Toy with you humans . . . play with the fates of man."

Orpheus was almost in tears. " Then I have lost my beloved for ever . . ."

Eurydice glared at him. "You don't hold out well under pressure, do you?"

"No!" cried Perce. "Stand up and be counted. You don't need a lyre – you can still sing!"

Orpheus drew himself up proudly. "Yes. Yes, you're right, I can. I will. Hades, I will sing for the release of my beloved." He cleared his throat, coughed self-consciously, threw his head back and warbled:

"Please release her, let her go . . .!"

Persephone blanched and dropped her secateurs. Perce winced. Maybe Orpheus did need his lyre after all.

Hades shook his head. "You'll have to do a lot better than that."

Orpheus tried again:

"She's the one I want – ooh, ooh, ooh!"

Eurydice groaned. "Oh, per-leeease . . ."

*"Tragedy – when your lyre has gone and you can't
  go on . . ."*

Eddie had his fingers in his ears. "That song is a tragedy, if you ask me."

Hades waved dismissively. "Next!"

Orpheus put his head in his hands. "It's no good without my lyre!"

Hades gave him a triumphant grin. "Then you have failed and must leave my realm without Eurydice."

"Wait!" yelled Perce. In the startled silence that followed, she turned to the boys. "Listen – we promised to help Orpheus get his girl back. What he needs is a crew."

Well'ard, Eddie and Andy gawped at Perce. "Where are you going to find one of those down here?" demanded Andy. Then he caught Perce's look. "Oh, no, Perce! If you think we're going to show ourselves up . . ."

"C'mere!" Perce dragged the boys into a huddle. A hurried consultation followed . . .

And then, Perce shoved her protesting companions into line to form the first boy (and one girl) band to sing underground. "Okay, homies," she said. "Gimme that beat."

With Andy, Eddie and Well'ard beatboxing for the world, Perce started to rap for Eurydice's life . . .

"So many thoughts goin' thru my head,
    now I'm standin' down here in the land of the dead.
I see red, 'cos you got Eurydice
    and you won't let her go, how can that be?"

Orpheus took up the plea on his own account:

"Hades, I could'a set your soul on fire,
  If only I hadn't done busted my lyre,
So I'm beggin', I'm pleadin', I'm down on my knees,
  All I'm askin' you please, is to grant her release . . ."

Swaying and stamping to the beat, Perce, Andy,
Eddie and Well'ard joined in the chorus:

"Oh, Hades, Hades, what's it worth, to let the girl
  return to Earth?
Oh, Hades, Hades, please be nice, let us take this girl
  to paradise . . ."

Hades scowled and stuffed his fingers in his ears.
Persephone, eyes closed, clicked her fingers and
swayed to the beat. Andy took up the lyric:

"See, you gotta understand, her life is in your hand
  We know we should be quakin' and not makin'
    demands . . ."

Eddie chimed in:

"But Hades, we ain't fools, we think we know the rules
  And keepin' this girl prisoner, hey, that ain't
    cool . . ."

Not to be outdone, Well'ard rasped:

"*Let her go, doe, she's done her time –*
  Oh, blimey, I can't think of a rhyme . . ."

Hurriedly, Perce cut in:

"*Hades, baby, cut her some slack,*
  and we solemnly swear . . ."

The others all joined in the chorus:

"*. . . we won't look back!*
Oh, Hades, Hades, what's it worth, to let the girl
  return to Earth?
Oh, Hades, Hades, please be nice, let us take this
  girl to paradise . . ."

Carried away by the music, Well'ard went into a breakdance, spinning on his chest, back and bottom like a large grubby gyroscope. His moves were so energetic that a buckle on the pack containing his souvenirs of London came undone. Still hanging by a single strap, the pack gaped open.

Oh, Hades, Hades, what's it worth, to let the girl
  return to Earth?

Oh, Hades, Hades, please be nice, let us take this girl to paradise . . ."

"**SILENCE!**" The Lord of the Underworld made an imperious gesture. Lightning crackled from his outstretched fingers and ricocheted around the rock walls. A thunderous blast of air hurled itself at the visitors, who abandoned the rap and crouched and shielded their eyes, fighting for breath. The tumult died down. Hades glared at the cowering supplicants with utter disdain. "And I thought Orpheus was bad! For subjecting me to that appalling noise, you can't have Eurydice back. Not now, not ever – never!"

Orpheus looked woebegone. Perce groaned. It was clear from Hades' expression that further argument was pointless. They had failed.

The ensuing silence was broken by a quiet little, 'Kerplink, kerplink, kerplink,' noise as something small and shiny dropped out of Well'ard's open pack and bounced across the stone floor, to come to rest at Persephone's feet. She bent and picked it up.

"What is this?" she asked in hushed tones.

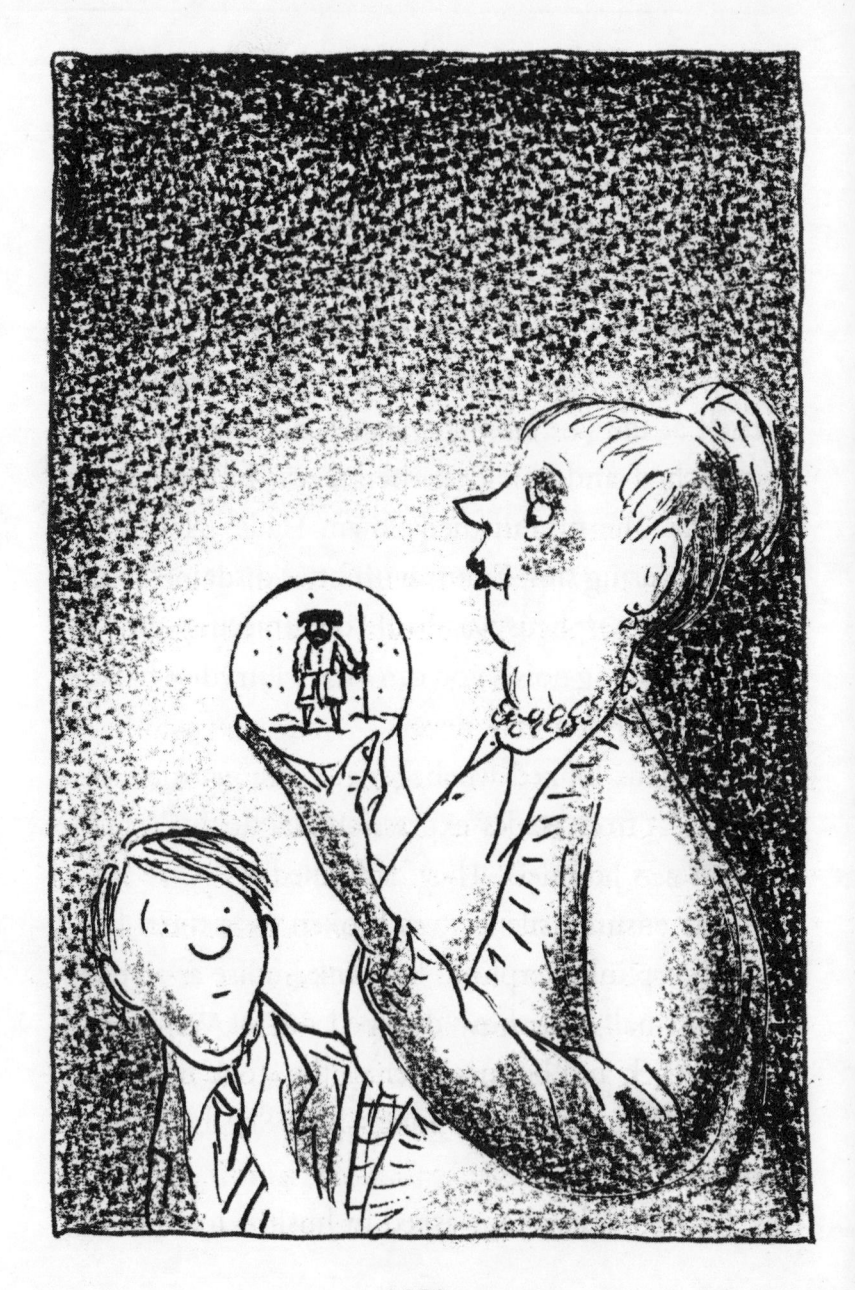

"Er – it's a glow-in-the-dark Beefeater snow globe, missus," said Well'ard. "I was takin' it home for my mum."

"It's beautiful," breathed Persephone. "Husband – see the pretty snowflakes. I haven't seen snow for thousands of years – see how it glows! And it's always dark down here." She turned the globe over and over in her hands, marvelling.

Perce stared at her. Maybe they hadn't lost after all. "It's yours," she said.

"Hang on!" Well'ard was furious. "That cost me a tenner! And I've already given up my MP3 player . . ."

"Well'ard," hissed Perce, "I'll buy you another Beefeater snow globe – a dozen Beefeater snow globes. Just belt up and leave this to me." Raising her voice, she continued. "Your majesty, we are happy to give you this rare and valuable gift – if your husband will agree to set Eurydice free."

"Whaaaat?" Hades let out a bellow of rage. "Restore this wench to her fool of a husband for some gaudy trinket? I won't do it!"

"Husband," said Persephone in warning tones.

"It's ridiculous! I am the King of the Dead, and

you seriously expect me to . . ."

"Husband!"

"Oh, all right, all right!" Hades glowered. "It's a deal. You get the girl, Perspehone gets – her whatever-it-is. Anything for a quiet life," he added, under his breath. "Now, get out of here! And don't look back!"

Perce grabbed Orpheus and Eurydice by the arm. "Let's do what the man says."

The companions fled from the palace, pursued by the moans of Hades and Persephone's shrill complaints: "Don't you raise your voice to me! You drag me down here, you never listen to a word I say, I should have listened to my mother, she tried to warn me about gods like you . . ."

As they hurried across the plain, Orpheus fell in beside Perce. "Is Eurydice following us? Perhaps I should check . . ."

"Don't look back!" warned Perce. "Why don't you just ask her? Come to think of it, why didn't you do that the last time?"

"I didn't think of that!"

"You der-brain," said Well'ard.

"Are you there my beloved?" called out Orpheus.

Eurydice's voice floated from the rear. "Yes, no thanks to you." Her voice rose in complaint. "I can't believe you just swapped me for some worthless bauble . . ."

"Oh yes – she's there," Perce reassured Orpheus. To herself, she muttered, "Some people are never satisfied."

They arrived at the station. A train stood at the empty platform, doors open, as though waiting for them.

Andy gave a whoop. "Great! Let's get home."

They piled in, and the doors closed. The train pulled away.

Perce took a seat facing the front of the carriage. "Face forwards," she warned the others. "Don't look back." She forced herself to obey her own instruction.

After some time, the train stopped. The doors opened. Perce read the sign on the station wall. "Olympia."

In hollow tones, Orpheus said, "I have a bad feeling about this . . ."

They set off down a corridor and found themselves at an escalator going upwards. With a shrug,

Perce stepped onto it. The others followed.

The escalator seemed endless. After a while the solid walls seemed to dissolve into vapour. Still, the escalator went on. Perce realised that they were now ascending through cloud – and then they burst through into bright sunlight. The escalator rose up and up – and there, in the distance, was a mountain peak, greater than any on Earth, surmounted by gleaming white halls and temples.

"Mount Olympus," breathed Orpheus from behind Perce. "Home of the immortal gods. This is not where we want to be . . ."

The escalator deposited them onto a stone pavement. White-robed gods and goddesses surveyed them dispassionately. A bearded figure wearing a laurel-wreath rose from a great marble throne.

"I am Zeus, father of the gods!" he bellowed in a voice that made the mountain tremble. He flung out a powerful arm. A thunderbolt detonated at the companions' feet and sent them staggering. "Quail, brief mortals!"

Chapter Eleven

OLYMPIC GAMES

Before Eddie could start rabbiting on about small birds, Perce spoke up. "Why?" she demanded.

The father of the gods blinked at her. "Sorry?"

"I said, 'Why?'" Perce jutted her chin and glared at Zeus. "What do you mean, telling us to quail? Why should we? Who d'you think you are, anyway?"

Well'ard tugged at her sleeve. "Er – Perce – that bloke with the thunderbolts looks like a bit of a tasty geezer. Be nice to him, okay?"

Zeus gave a roar of rage and detonated another thunderbolt. "I am Zeus, father of gods, terror of men! You will tremble and bow down before me!"

"No, we won't," Perce told him. Eddie gave a moan of terror. Orpheus and Eurydice closed their eyes, held on to each other and waited for the end. "From where I'm standing," Perce continued, "you're just some bloke in a bed-sheet. You look ridiculous."

"Yeah," said Andy, feeling he ought to support Perce (who couldn't help feeling that his defiance would have been more impressive if he hadn't been hiding behind her when he said it).

"Infamous mortal! Sacrilegious wretch!" A look of pain crossed Zeus's face. He gave a huge burp and knocked discontentedly at his ribs with a clenched fist. "Now look what you've done," he complained. "You've brought on my heartburn. Doctor Hippocrates keeps telling me not to get excited, it sets me off."

"Well, it's your own fault." The haughty-looking goddess sitting beside Zeus gave him an exasperated look. "All that ranting and raving and throwing thunderbolts about. Nobody's impressed." By now, several gods were snickering behind Zeus's back.

"But, Hera, my love," protested Zeus, "the dignity of my position . . ."

"To Hades with the dignity of your position! You're just throwing your weight about as usual. You ought to be ashamed."

"That's right," said Perce, encouraged. "Hades is in charge of the Underworld, not you. He let us all go, and then you brought us up here instead. Who gave you the right to interfere? You're just a big bully."

Orpheus looked up at Zeus's face, which was rapidly going purple, and said, "Well, that's about it for this life." Several of the gods were laughing out loud by now.

"And another thing," Perce went on, before the enraged father of the gods could speak. "What about all the characters from myth that have been turning up in our world – Medusa, Odysseus, the Minotaur and the rest? I'll bet that was you, wasn't it?"

"Ssssh!" There was a sudden look of panic in Zeus's face. All his bluster was gone. He gave Perce a beseeching look and silently mouthed, "Not in front of the wife . . ."

"What's this?" demanded Hera in a tone that made Zeus cringe. "What have I told you about causing chaos in the world of men?"

"It's a lie! I never . . ."

"Zeus!"

"Oh, all right, all right. A man's got to have a hobby, my sweet," Zeus wheedled. "Just a little bit of fun, to while away the empty centuries."

"You silly old fool." Hera's voice was no longer angry, but sad. She turned to Perce. "You see, mortal girl, the trouble with being an eternal god is – that one is eternal. And the trouble with eternity is – it's such an awfully long time." She sighed. "A few thousand years ago it was different: it was fun! We all had our favourite heroes and we'd send them off on quests and whatnot . . ."

Zeus chuckled reminiscently. 'Remember Heracles? He was one of mine. You never liked him. You arranged it so he had to do all those labours."

"Yes. They were supposed to keep him out of trouble." Hera gave Perce and Andy a knowing look. "Your own ancestors – Perseus and Andromeda – had help from the gods Hermes and Athena." A god wearing winged sandals and a mischievous grin winked at Perce, and a goddess wearing full armour gave her a brief nod.

"Yes, but Perseus and Andromeda wouldn't have needed help if the gods hadn't got them into that mess in the first place, would they?" Perce wasn't in a mood for being reasonable. "Human beings aren't *counters* in some stupid board game! We're not around just to help you keep the *score*."

Zeus tugged at Hera's gown. "Shall I smite her with thunderbolts, my love?"

For a moment, it seemed from Hera's angry look that she would agree. Perce felt her heart thudding against her ribs. She heard Andy say, "We're behind you, Perce." Turning, she saw him, Eddie and Well'ard backing away. "Quite a long *way* behind you, actually . . ."

But then, Hera's anger seemed to fade. She shook her head. "No. She's right, of course." She turned back to Perce. "The truth of the matter is, we're bored. Nobody believes in us any more. I suppose I can't really blame my Zeussy for trying to liven things up and get people's attention by bringing a few monsters and heroes back to life."

Zeussy? thought Perce. Aloud, she said, "That's the point. You're not needed anymore. This is the twenty-first century." Ignoring the dissatisfied rumbles all around her, she ploughed on, "People used to need gods because they didn't understand how the world was created or how it worked, so they needed stories to make sense of everything."

Andy nodded. "Even if the stories were wrong.

And they needed you to be in charge of it all, so that when things went wrong, at least they'd know that you could put it all right. If they prayed hard enough, and sacrificed enough goats and chickens . . ."

Perce gave the gods a disapproving look. "Even though you hardly ever did."

"The trouble is," one of the gods said apologetically, "if you answered one person's prayer, you'd have to answer everybody's prayer . . ."

Perce ignored this. "But now, we know that earthquakes and volcanic eruptions are caused by . . ." She clicked her tongue in annoyance. "What are they caused by, Eddie?"

"Continental plates rubbing together."

"Yeah, what he said. They're not the anger of the gods."

"That's right," added Andy. "And we know that fire wasn't stolen from you, either – any idiot can make it with two sticks and a lot of patience."

"And the sun isn't some boy-racer taking his chariot for a spin . . ." Perce spread her hands in appeal. "You've had your day, okay? It's about time you just left people alone."

The gods looked at each other and shuffled their feet. Zeus hurled a thunderbolt, but it was clear to everyone that his heart wasn't in it, and it went off with a sad little 'blat!' noise. Hera gave her husband a frosty look and whispered urgently in his ear. Zeus's brow darkened; he seemed about to protest, but if so he thought better of it.

"Oh, all right, all right." The father of the gods shifted uneasily on his throne. He continued sulkily, "Having discussed the matter with my wife and reconsidered my position, my dread sentence is..." Hera cleared her throat loudly. Zeus gave an ill-tempered shrug, and waved a dismissive hand towards Perce, Andy, Well'ard and Eddie. "You four can all go back to Earth."

"And . . .?" prompted Hera.

Zeus rolled his eyes. "And I won't send any more monsters or characters from Greek myth to plague you." He glared at Hera. "Is that enough? Would you like me to give them the chiton off my back as well?"

Andy and Eddie stepped forward to Perce and took an arm each. "Okay, fine, well done, Perce." Andy was clearly desperate to get away while the going was good. "Say thank you to the nice gods and goddesses, and we'll be on our way . . ."

Perce shook them off. "What about Orpheus and Eurydice?" she demanded. "You haven't said what you're going to do with them . . ."

But this time, she had gone too far. The gods and goddesses of Olympus stepped forward, muttering angrily. Hera's eyes flashed. Zeus rose out of his throne in wrath.

"Impudent girl!" he roared. "I am chief of the immortal gods! Orpheus and Eurydice are subject to me – and if I am not allowed to interfere in the affairs of men, you certainly have no right to meddle in the affairs of Olympus! Begone!"

The gods roared with anger and shook their fists. Cracks appeared in the mountainside, from which poured satyrs, ferocious maenads, wild women with claws like daggers, and bat-winged furies, screeching with rage.

Eddie gazed, horror-stricken, at the face of Zeus in his wrath. "We're quailing," he squeaked, "we're quailing!" He grabbed Perce by the arm and dragged her away. "Leg it! And don't look back!"

Andy and Well'ard followed Perce and Eddie in

headlong retreat down the mountain. Thunderbolts detonated around them. The satyrs, maenads and furies tore at their hair and snapped at their heels. They staggered as, with a great jolt, the mountain itself convulsed, and the whole side of Olympus gave way above them. The landslide tore in pursuit, destroying everything in its path, seeking to engulf the fleeing companions in a thundering torrent of earth and stone.

Chapter Twelve

STAR QUALITY

Perce and the others pounded onto the station platform seconds ahead of the howling destruction that was pursuing them, and threw themselves into the waiting train. A robotic voice intoned, "Please stand clear of the closing doors . . ."

"We're clear! Close them!" Perce gasped in horror as the landslide reached out to crush them – but at that moment, the doors slid together and the train pulled away. It shot into the tunnel just as the roaring deluge of earth obliterated the platform. Clouds of dust billowed into the tunnel, only to fall behind and disappear as the train gathered speed.

Perce slumped into a seat and mopped her face. "That was close!"

Andy, Well'ard and Eddie had been rendered speechless by their flight down the mountain. They could only nod.

The boys had almost recovered their breath by

the time the train pulled into another station. The doors opened and four heads peered cautiously out.

Perce pointed at the sign on the wall. "Victoria."

"Does that mean we've won?" asked Eddie.

Cautiously, Perce led the way to the exit, expecting that at any moment another creature from the Underworld would leap out at them and do everything it could to make their lives exciting. But nothing happened. At the exit, they found a lift waiting with its doors open.

"Going down, I'll bet," said Perce grimly.

As soon as they were all inside, the doors closed and, to Perce's immense relief, pressure on her feet told her that this time, at long, long last, they had found a lift that was going up. She could have wept with joy, if she hadn't wanted to look soppy in front of the boys.

The lift stopped with a jerk and the doors opened. They stepped out into a crowded Underground station concourse.

"Yes!" Andy punched the air. Eddie and Well'ard exchanged high fives. Perce gave a huge sigh of relief – and then rocked back on her heels with a startled cry as a terrible face appeared – a face out of a ghoul's worst nightmares. A face twisted and convulsed by muscles that twitched uncontrollably. A ghastly face with bloodshot, staring eyes and a leering, slobbering mouth . . .

"Where the hell have you been?" screeched Mr Latimer.

Perce stared at the incandescent teacher. "Funny you should say that, sir . . ."

"You've been missing for hours!" Mr Latimer clenched and unclenched his fists as if barely controlling his desire to tear Perce limb from limb. "I've had half the Metropolitan Police out looking for you!"

"Sorry, sir," Perce managed at last, "we got a bit lost . . .in the Underground. That's it. We took the wrong train, you see, and . . ."

"How did you know you'd find us here? And where did you just spring from, anyway?"

"From the lift, just here . . ." Perce looked around, and her voice tailed away. Behind her was an unbroken wall of white tiles. There was no lift.

Well'ard came to Perce's rescue. "Up the escalator, sir. And we knew where you were 'cos we did what you told us – we asked a policeman." He gave Mr Latimer a dazzling smile of transparent honesty.

Syreeta gave Well'ard a disbelieving look. "You asked a policeman?"

Claire Greene sniffed. "I bet he's lying, sir."

"Thank you, girls, that will do." Mr Latimer glowered at the returnees. "I'll deal with you four later." He turned to the rest of Perce's chattering, grinning classmates and raised his hand. "Forward!"

Perce was silent, lost in thought, as the group threaded its way through crowded streets. She didn't become aware of her surroundings until she found herself clattering down a sloping walkway, which led to a floating platform on the river Thames. "Where are we?" she asked.

"Haven't you been listening?" said Eddie. "Westminster Pier." He pointed. "We're going down to Greenwich on that boat, so's we can visit the Royal Observatory."

"What fun," said Perce listlessly.

As they cruised down the river, with Mr Latimer pointing out allegedly interesting landmarks, Andy muttered to Perce, "What are you face-aching about? We got out of the Underworld! We're still alive! You ought to be dancing around handing out funny hats and party poppers."

"I know," said Perce. "We got out. But what about Orpheus and Eurydice? We promised to help them, and we left them on Olympus. Zeus might have done anything to them – he might have sent them *both* back to the Underworld." She gave the Tower of London a gloomy look and sighed. "Oh well, there's no point in worrying about it. I don't suppose we'll ever know."

Perce was silent all the way to Greenwich. During the slog uphill through the park, while most of the group were complaining about their poor feet, she said nothing. But even in her abstracted mood, she couldn't fail to notice the buzz among the crowd when they reached the Royal Observatory and were shepherded into the queue for the planetarium.

Mr Latimer was showing off his knowledge, as usual. "Now, for those of you who have not visited a planetarium before; you will shortly be entering the dome, upon which will be projected images of the night sky . . ." Ignoring the groans from the less astronomically-minded members of the group, he continued, "I understand from Observatory staff that we are very fortunate: this is a new presentation, and you will be among the first to witness a fascinating discovery which I'm sure you'll all find tremendously exciting."

Glum faces around Perce indicated that other members of the group seriously doubted this, but they all trooped obediently into the auditorium and settled themselves into their seats. Then the lights around the dome darkened (*at least, Perce thought, if it's too boring, I can always go to sleep*) and a field of stars appeared above their heads. The chattering of the audience died away.

"Before we begin our usual tour of the night sky . . ." Perce listened to the amplified voice and felt her eyelids beginning to droop ". . . we want to share with you an astounding new discovery. Astronomers have announced the appearance of a new constellation in the vicinity of Lyra – the lyre." Perce sat bolt upright. "Scientists are unable to explain the sudden appearance of an entire star system in what has been, up to now, regarded as an almost blank section of sky." Perce felt a mo-

ment's vertigo as the star field expanded, as if she were in a spaceship approaching it at warp factor whoosh, then steadied to focus on a pattern of stars that looked somehow familiar.

"In keeping with the practice of ancient astronomers of seeing divine figures among the stars," the commentary continued, "and naming them after gods and creatures of myth, the discoverers of the new constellation have decided to call it 'Orpheus and Eurydice'."

Perce caught her breath as a network of lines appeared, connecting the stars – and then more lines, filling in the detail, white on black, like the patterns on a Greek vase, until the full picture was revealed. And there was Orpheus, strumming his lyre. Beside him stood Eurydice, her hand on his shoulder. As Perce gazed, spellbound, the star that lay in the centre of Orpheus's right eye twinkled. It might have been a wink.

Ignoring the startled whispers of Andy, Eddie and Well'ard, Perce smiled happily – and settled herself down in her seat for a nap. She felt she'd earned it.

It had been one hell of a day.

WHO'S WHO?

Gods, Heroes and Monsters of Ancient Greece

Andromeda – A maiden rescued by Perseus from a sea monster.

Cerberus – The three-headed dog who guards the gates to the Underworld.

Charon – The ferryman who takes the souls of the dead across the River Acheron to the Underworld.

Eurydice – Wife of Orpheus. She was bitten by a snake and became a prisoner in the Underworld.

Hades – Lord of the Dead, and ruler of the Underworld.

Hera – Zeus's wife.

Medusa the Gorgon – Snake-haired monster who could kill with a look.

Orpheus – The greatest poet and musician of Ancient Greece, whose first attempt to rescue his wife Eurydice from the Underworld ended in disaster.

Persephone – Wife of Hades and queen of the Underworld.

Perseus – The hero who defeated Medusa (with a little help from the gods).

Zeus – The father of the Gods, ruler of the sky. Brother to Poseidon, ruler of the sea, and to Hades, ruler of the Underworld.

About the authors

STEVE BARLOW was born in Crewe but now lives in Somerset with his wife and cats. After working as a puppeteer, refuse collector and laundry-van driver, he became a teacher of performing arts, before turning to full-time writing.

STEVE SKIDMORE was born in Leicester. He trained as a teacher and met Steve Barlow at a school in Nottingham nearly twenty years ago. They began writing plays for their students and haven't looked back.

'THE 2 STEVES' are Britain's most popular writing double-act for young people, specialising in comedy and adventure. They perform regularly in schools and libraries, delighting audiences of all ages.

To find out more about 'THE 2 STEVES', visit their website at *www.the2steves.net*

More *myths* from the 2 Steves

STONE ME!

by *Steve Barlow & Steve Skidmore*

Illustrated by Tony Ross

ISBN 1-903015-43-X £4.99

When a new supply teacher called Ms Dusa turns up at the school wearing a large turban over her hair, Perce and Andy get suspicious. After several children get turned into stone the duo realise they are right, this is indeed Medusa come into the 21st Century. As none of the grown ups seem to rumble as to what is happening, Perce and Andy decide that action needs to be taken and they are the ones to take it!

A TOUCH OF WIND!

by *Steve Barlow & Steve Skidmore*

Illustrated by Tony Ross

ISBN 1-903015-56-1 £4.99

Look what the wind's blown in!

When Odysseus left the Siege of Troy for his home in Greece, he wasn't planning a detour via Bogmouth-on-Sylt.

He's already put the wind up Major Eyeswater. Perce and Andy are trying to get him back where he belongs but they're making heavy weather of it.

The Voyage of Odysseus as it really happened!

MIND THE DOOR!

by Steve Barlow & Steve Skidmore

Illustrated by Tony Ross

ISBN 1-903015-49-9   £4.99

The new school caretaker has Perce worried. Not just because he's got a body like King Kong's big brother. Nor because he wears a trendy nose-ring. It's just that – well, he seems like a bit of a bully. Andy couldn't care less. He thinks Mr O'Taur is the best thing sinced microwave popcorn. But then kids start to go missing from Mr O'Taur's gym club. And when the terrible secret of the Labyrinth is revealed, Perce, Andy, Well'ard and Eddie Johnson realise that they have the bull by the horns and their lives are hanging by a thread . . . (Well, okay, a loo-roll . . .)

VLAD THE DRAC

by Ann Jungman

ISBN 1-903015-22-7   £4.99

When Judy and Paul get talked into bringing a tiny vampire they meet on holiday back to England they have no idea the trouble they are storing up . . . Vlad may be a vegetarian and harmless but he does like to wander round the house and can't resist pretending to be a scary bloodsucker. How long can Judy and Paul keep him a secret?